# More Experiences Unpacked: Relevant Short Stories

*The TNT Group*

# Prelude

***"More Experiences Unpacked"** by The TNT Group is an excellent short storybook for ESL learners and young people interested in learning about current events and daily life issues. The book aims to shed light on the challenges that people from all walks of life often face with its diverse range of characters and real-life scenarios, "More Experiences Unpacked" is a must-read for anyone looking to gain a better understanding of the complexities of life.*

**Life Is Like A Slice Of Cake**

Sarah loved nothing more than baking cakes. She would spend hours in the kitchen, experimenting with different ingredients and decorating techniques, always striving to create the perfect sweet treat. One day, as she was carefully mixing a batch of batter, she began to reflect on how similar life was to her beloved cakes. Just like a cake, life had its ups and downs. Sometimes, things went smoothly and the end result was something beautiful and delicious. Other times, the batter was too thick or the oven was too hot, and the cake was a disaster.

Through it all, Sarah knew that the key to making a great cake was to keep trying. She would never give up, even when things didn't go as planned. She would adjust the recipe, try new techniques, and keep experimenting until she got it right. In the same way, Sarah realized that the key to living a fulfilling life was to keep trying, even when things didn't go as planned. She knew that there would be times when things would be difficult and she would make mistakes, but she also knew that by staying persistent and never giving up, she would be able to create something beautiful and delicious, just like her cakes.

Sarah went on to become a successful pastry chef, known for her delicious cakes and her never-say-die attitude. And she always remembered the lesson she learned in the kitchen: that just like a cake, life is sweetest when you put your heart and soul into it.

**Generation Gap**

An old man named Robert lived in the same small town for his entire life. He had seen the town change and grow over the years, but he still held on to the traditional values and customs of his youth.

A young couple named Anna and Jake moved into the town, eager to start a new chapter in their lives. They were full of new ideas and energy, and they quickly became involved in the community, working to make the town a better place. Despite their good intentions, Robert couldn't help but feel a sense of resentment towards the young couple. He couldn't understand their ways and felt they were trying to change everything he had grown to love about his town. He often found himself clashing with them, and the more they tried to involve him in their plans, the more resistant he became.

Anna and Jake, on the other hand, couldn't understand why Robert was so opposed to change. They saw him as stubborn and unwilling to consider new perspectives. They didn't realize that Robert's resistance was rooted in a deep-seated fear of losing the traditions and values that had defined his life. As time went on, the three of them found themselves at a standstill, unable to bridge the gap between their generations. But one day, a crisis hit the town and everyone had to come together to solve it. Robert, Anna, and Jake found themselves working side by side, and in that moment, they realized that despite their differences, they all had the same goal: to make their town a better place.

Through this experience, Robert came to understand that the new ideas and energy that Anna and Jake brought were not a threat to the traditions and values he held dear, but rather an opportunity to grow and evolve, in turn, coming to understand and appreciate the wisdom and experience that Robert brought to the table.

The three of them worked together, combining their different perspectives and experiences, to make their town a better place for all and they realized that the generation gap was not something to be feared, but rather an opportunity for growth and learning.

**Theft or Stealing**

Craig, despite his friendly nature, had a problem: he loved to steal. Whether it was candy from the corner store or toys from his classmates, and couldn't resist the thrill of taking things that didn't belong to him.

One day, Craig decided to steal something big. He had his eye on a shiny new bicycle that belonged to the richest kid in town, as he knew that if he could steal that bicycle, he would be the coolest kid in school. That night, Craig snuck out of his house and made his way to the rich kid's neighborhood, crept through the streets, avoiding streetlights and barking dogs. Finally, he arrived at the rich kid's house where he saw the bicycle sitting in the driveway, just waiting for him to take it.

Craig reached out and grabbed the handlebars of the bicycle. But just as he was about to take off, he heard a voice behind him. "Hey! What do you think you're doing?"

It was the rich kid, who had come outside to investigate the noise. Craig froze, unsure of what to do. "I-I'm sorry," he stammered. "I just wanted to borrow the bike for a little while." The rich kid stared at him for a moment, then shook his head. "You can't just take something that doesn't belong to you," he said. "That's stealing, and it's wrong."

Craig felt a pang of guilt in his chest being that he knew the rich kid was right. He let go of the bicycle and hung his head in shame. "I'm sorry," he repeated. The rich kid softened. "It's okay," he said. "Everyone makes mistakes. But you need to understand that stealing is never the answer. If you want something, you have to work for it or ask for it."

Craig nodded, understanding. From that day on, he never stole again. He worked hard and saved his money, and eventually, he was able to buy his own bicycle, and it felt a hundred times better than stealing one ever could have.

## COVID

A mysterious virus called COVID-19 appeared out of the blue. It quickly spread across the globe, causing widespread illness and panic. Governments implemented lockdowns, shuttering businesses, and causing widespread unemployment. People were afraid to leave their homes, and those who could work from home did so, while essential workers risked their health every day to keep society functioning.

Despite initial resistance from some, masks became a symbol of solidarity in the fight against the virus. Scientists and researchers worked tirelessly to develop a vaccine, and after much effort, one was finally approved and distributed globally. Slowly but surely, life began to return to a new normal, with widespread vaccination and cautious optimism for a brighter future.

The effects of the pandemic lingered as the global economy struggled to recover, and many people were still out of work. Mental health took a toll on individuals, as they grappled with isolation and the loss of loved ones.

However, the pandemic also brought out the best in humanity. Neighbors came together to support one another, volunteer organizations worked to help those in need, and people learned to appreciate the simple joys in life. The experience of the pandemic was a reminder to cherish each day and the people in our lives.

And so, while the virus may have temporarily changed the world, it could not diminish the spirit and resilience of the human race. The story of COVID-19 will always be remembered as a testament to the strength and determination of the human spirit.

**Crypto or Cryptocurrency**

In a world not so different from our own, there lived a brilliant young programmer named Alex. He had always been fascinated by the idea of decentralized currency and had spent years studying the technology behind it.

While browsing the internet one day, he stumbled upon a new cryptocurrency called Bitcoin. He was immediately intrigued and decided to dive deeper into the world of digital currencies. As he learned more about Bitcoin and other cryptocurrencies, he realized that they had the potential to change the world. He became determined to create his own cryptocurrency that would be even better than Bitcoin.

He spent months working tirelessly on his project, pouring all of his knowledge and skills into it. Finally, after much hard work, he succeeded in creating a revolutionary new cryptocurrency called Ethereum. Ethereum was faster, more secure, and more versatile than any other digital currency that had come before it. It quickly gained popularity among tech enthusiasts and investors alike, and its value began to soar.

Alex became an overnight millionaire, and Ethereum became one of the most valuable cryptocurrencies in the world. He used his newfound wealth to invest in other promising crypto projects, and soon became a major player in the industry.

As the years went by, Ethereum continued to gain mainstream acceptance and its value continued to rise. Alex's early investment in the crypto space had paid off, and he lived a life of luxury and financial freedom, but he never forgot his passion for decentralized currency and the potential it had to change the world. He continued to work on Ethereum and other crypto projects, always striving to make them better and more accessible to everyone.

And so, the world of cryptocurrency continued to evolve and grow, bringing financial freedom and innovation to people all over the globe.

**Promise**

Paul was known throughout the neighborhood for his kind heart and his ability to keep his promises, no matter what. The town was struck by a severe drought. The residents were worried as their crops were failing and they had no water to drink. Paul knew that he had to do something to help, so he set out on a journey to find a solution.

After many days of wandering through the forest, Paul came across a clear stream that flowed down from the mountains and knew that this was the answer to the neighbor's problems, so he made a promise to himself to bring the water back to the town, no matter what it took. Paul set out to build a system of canals and dams that would bring the water from the stream to the neighborhood, It was a difficult task, but he never gave up, working tirelessly, day and night until finally, the water began to flow into the village.

The residents were overjoyed and they thanked Paulk for keeping his promise. Onwards, the village never suffered from a drought again, and Paul's reputation as a man of his word was cemented forever. Years passed and Paul grew old, but he never forgot his promise to the town. He made sure that the water system was always maintained and that the residents always had the water they needed. When he passed away, the town erected a statue in his honor, a reminder to all of the importance of keeping one's promises.

**Culture**

Emily had always dreamed of traveling the world, saved up for years, and finally decided to take the plunge and spend a year abroad in a small remote town in Japan. At first, everything was wonderful. The people were kind and welcoming, the food was delicious, and the culture was fascinating. Emily quickly fell in love with the country and its way of life.

However, as the weeks went by, Emily began to experience a sense of unease. She found herself feeling lost and out of place in this new environment. She didn't understand the customs and traditions, and she struggled to communicate with the locals. She missed her family and friends back home, and she felt like an outsider in her new home.

Emily felt overwhelmed and isolated, and she started to question her decision to come to Japan. She didn't know if she would be able to make it through the year, but one day, she met a kind and patient woman named Hiroko who helped her to understand the culture and customs. Hiroko taught her how to navigate the public transportation system, how to order food at restaurants, and how to communicate with the locals. She also introduced Emily to new friends and helped her to find a sense of community in the village.

Through Hiroko's guidance, Emily began to understand and appreciate the culture more and more. She found joy in learning the language, and she became more comfortable communicating with the people in her village. She realized that culture shock was a normal part of the experience of living in a foreign country and that with patience and an open mind, she could overcome it. Emily's year in Japan was not easy, but it was one of the most rewarding experiences of her life. She returned home with a newfound appreciation for different cultures and a desire to continue traveling and learning about the world

**BOSS**

There were two bosses at a company, one was favorable and one was lousy. The good boss was named Molly and she was the manager of a small team of employees at a marketing agency. Molly was always fair and kind to her team, and she was always willing to listen to their ideas and concerns, making sure that her team had everything they needed to do their jobs well, she always recognized their hard work and accomplishments.

The bad boss, on the other hand, Jim the manager of a different team at the same agency, was always short-tempered, demanding, never gave positive feedback, and was always quick to point out mistakes. He would often belittle his team in front of others and would take credit for their work.

The employees who worked for Molly were happy and motivated, and they were always willing to go above and beyond to help the company succeed. They knew that their hard work would be recognized and appreciated. On the other hand, the employees who worked for Jim were unhappy and demotivated, and they often dreaded coming to work because they knew that no matter how hard they worked, they would never be able to please him.

The company would eventually merge the two teams, and the employees who had worked for Jim were finally able to experience the positive and supportive work environment that Molly had created, where they thrived under her leadership and the team as a whole became one of the most successful in the company. The employees who had worked for Jim were grateful to have been given the opportunity to work with a good boss and they made sure to thank Molly for her leadership and support.

It was clear in the end that a good boss like Molly could make a huge difference in the lives of her employees and in the success of a company. On the other hand, a bad boss like Jim could make work a miserable experience for everyone. The story serves as a reminder that the way a boss treats their employees can have a profound impact on their happiness and performance.

**Weather**

In a faraway country, the weather was always a topic of conversation among the locals. The winters were long and harsh, with heavy snowfall blocking the mountain passes for months at a time. The villagers would huddle around their fireplaces, sipping hot cocoa and telling stories to pass the time.

But with spring came a change in the weather. The snow began to melt, and the mountain passes opened up once more. The locals would venture out of their homes, taking in the fresh air and the warm sun on their faces. The flowers started to bloom, and the birds returned to the village, filling the air with their songs.

Summer brought even more warmth and sun, and the locals would spend their days swimming in the nearby lake and picnicking in the meadows. The crops in the fields grew tall and strong, and the farmers' bellies were full of delicious fruits and vegetables.

But as the leaves began to change color in the fall, the locals knew that the weather was about to take a turn for the worse. The winds picked up, and the rain started to fall. The villagers would gather around the fire once more, listening to the howling wind and the pitter-patter of the rain on the roof, however, they knew that no matter how harsh the weather may be, it was all a part of the cycle of life. They learned to be grateful for the warmth and the sun, the rain and the snow, for they knew that without it, their country would not be the same.

**Media Manipulators**

There was a powerful and wealthy tycoon who controlled all forms of media in the Island. The tycoon, known as the Czar, was determined to maintain his power and influence over the people at all costs.

To achieve this goal, the Czar hired a team of expert manipulators to control the narrative in the media. They worked tirelessly to shape public opinion and control the flow of information. They spread false rumors and planted fake stories in the newspapers, on television, and on social media, silencing anyone who dared to speak out against the Czar or his regime.

The people of the Island unaware of the manipulation believed everything they saw and heard in the media. They trusted the Czar and his government, and many even supported his policies and actions however, a brave and determined journalist named Alice uncovered the truth about the media manipulation. She was determined to expose the Czar's deceit and bring justice to the people, working tirelessly to gather evidence and interview sources, despite the many obstacles and dangers she faced.

Eventually, Alice's hard work paid off, as she was able to publish her findings in a major newspaper, and the truth about Czar's media manipulation was revealed to the world. The people were shocked and outraged by the deception, and they began to demand change.

The Czar, realizing that he could no longer maintain his grip on power, stepped down from the throne. The Island was plunged into chaos and turmoil as the people struggled to rebuild their society and create a new government based on transparency and democracy. Alice, the brave journalist, became a hero to the people, and her legacy lived on as a symbol of truth and justice.

**Life is School**

Mike had just started his first day of school. Everything was new and exciting to him, from the colorful classrooms to the friendly faces of his classmates, so he was eager to learn and soak up as much knowledge as possible.

As the days passed, Mike began to realize that school was a lot like life. Just as he had to attend classes and complete assignments to pass his grades, in life he would have to work hard and achieve his goals to be successful. He also learned that just as in school, in life there were challenges and obstacles to overcome. But, just as his teachers were there to guide him and help him when he needed it, he would have a support system of friends and family to help him through the tough times in life.

As Mike grew older and progressed through school, he came to understand that the skills he was learning in the classroom, such as problem-solving, communication, and time management, were essential for success not just in school, but in life as well.

Ultimately, Mike graduated from school and went on to lead a successful and fulfilling life, applying the lessons he had learned in the classroom to the challenges and opportunities he faced in the real world. He realized that just as school was a journey, life was too and the two were not so different after all. He was grateful for the time he spent in school, as it had prepared him well for the journey ahead.

**Share**

A generous bear named Bert. Bert loved nothing more than to share his bountiful harvest of honey and berries with his friends and neighbors. A young rabbit named Rabbit came to Bert's cave, looking for help. Rabbit's family had fallen on hard times, and they had no food to eat. Bert didn't hesitate to share his food with Rabbit and his family. He gave them all the honey and berries they could carry, and even invited them to come back and forage in his cave whenever they needed.

Word of Bert's generosity soon spread throughout the village, and more and more animals began to come to him for help. Bert never turned anyone away, always happy to share his food and resources with those in need. As the years passed, the village prospered and grew stronger, thanks in large part to Bert's selfless spirit of sharing. And Bert, too, was happy and fulfilled, knowing that he had made a positive impact on the lives of his friends and neighbors.

The village and its animal inhabitants came to be known as a sharing and caring community, they were all happy and lived in harmony. In the end, Bert's kind and generous nature were beneficial not only to him but also to the entire village, and his legacy of sharing lived on for many generations.

**Ethics**

Jason was a curious and adventurous child, always eager to explore the world around him, would often wander deep into the forest, where he discovered many wonders, but also many dangers. One day exploring a particularly dense part of the forest, he came across a beautiful, sparkling gem. Jason was amazed by the gem's beauty and picked it up, intending to take it back to the village as a treasure. As he turned to leave, he heard a faint, pitiful cry coming from a nearby bush.

Jason walked towards the bush and discovered a small, injured bird lying on the ground. The bird had a broken wing and was unable to fly. Jason immediately knew what he had to do. He gently picked up the bird and carefully carried it back to the village, where he found a kind old woman who was able to heal the bird's wing.

As the bird flew away, healthy and strong once again, Jason realized that the true treasure was not the sparkling gem he had found earlier, but the life of the innocent bird. From that day on, Jason understood the importance of morals and the value of compassion and kindness. He knew that true riches were not found in material possessions, but in the well-being of others.

Jason lived his life with this newfound understanding, always putting the needs of others before his own and spreading kindness and compassion wherever he went. He became a beloved member of the village, and his legacy lived on long after he was gone, inspiring others to lead lives of compassion and morality.

**Service: Company A versus Company B**

Company A had poor customer service. They didn't answer phone calls or emails promptly, and when they did, their representatives were rude and unhelpful. They didn't take responsibility for their mistakes and didn't seem to care about their customers' satisfaction. Company B had excellent customer service. They answered phone calls and emails promptly and were always willing to help. Their representatives were friendly and knowledgeable, and they went above and beyond to make sure their customers were happy. They took responsibility for their mistakes and always worked to find a solution.

A customer had a problem with a product they had purchased from Company A. They called the customer service line, but no one answered. They sent an email, but it went unanswered. Frustrated and fed up, the customer decided to reach out to Company B, who they had heard had great customer service.

The customer service representative at Company B listened patiently to the customer's problem and immediately took action to resolve it. They apologized for the inconvenience and offered a refund or replacement for the faulty product. The customer was extremely satisfied with the level of service they received and decided to become a loyal customer of Company B from that day forward.

Word of Company B's excellent customer service spread quickly, and soon, many customers who had previously dealt with Company A's poor service switched to Company B. As a result, Company B's business grew and prospered, while Company A's declined. In the end, it was clear that good customer service can make all the difference.

### Gamble

Tom fascinated by the thrill of gambling, would often spend his evenings at the local casino, playing slot machines and poker. He was convinced that he had a knack for it and that one day he would strike it rich.

Tom as time went by decided to try his luck at the high-stakes poker table after he had saved up for months to be able to afford the buy-in and was determined to make a big profit. As the night went on, Tom's stack of chips grew larger and larger, and soon he found himself in the lead.

The final hand of the night was dealt, and Tom was dealt a pair of aces, which he knew was a strong hand, so he bet big, and to his surprise, all of the other players folded. Tom had won the pot and with it, a large sum of money. Ecstatic with his win, Tom decided to quit while he was ahead. He cashed in his chips and left the casino, feeling like a true winner.

As time passed, Tom found that the thrill of gambling was too hard to resist. He would return to the casino and slowly but surely, he lost all of his winnings and more, and realized that his love for gambling had turned into an addiction, and it was slowly ruining his life. He knew he needed to stop, but it was a hard habit to break. In the end, he sought help and was able to overcome his addiction and regain control of his life, but he learned a valuable lesson about the dangers of gambling and the importance of knowing when to quit.

## Solar

In a far-off galaxy, there was a solar system much like our own. It was made up of eight planets that orbited around a bright, burning star we call the sun. The first four planets were small and rocky, much like Earth, but the last four were large and gaseous.

A team of brilliant scientists and engineers from the planet Earth set out on a journey to explore this solar system. They built a spacecraft that was capable of traveling at incredible speeds and was equipped with all the latest technology. The journey began with a trip to the nearest planet, Mercury. It was a barren and inhospitable world, but the team was able to gather valuable data and samples before moving on to Venus. This planet was covered in thick clouds, and the team had to use special instruments to study the surface.

After visiting Venus, the team traveled to Mars, the fourth planet from the sun. This planet was of particular interest to the team because it had signs of water and possibly even life. The team spent several weeks on Mars, gathering data and taking samples before returning to Earth. Next, they visited Jupiter, the largest planet in the solar system. It was a massive gas giant with raging storms and massive red spots. The team flew their spacecraft through the planet's thick atmosphere and even got a glimpse of its beautiful rings.

Saturn was the next stop on their journey, and it was just as breathtaking as Jupiter. The team was able to get a close-up view of the planet's famous rings and even landed on one of its many moons. After Saturn, the team visited Uranus and Neptune, both of which were cold and distant planets. They were able to gather valuable data and samples before returning to Earth.

Finally, the team visited Pluto, the last planet in the solar system. It was a small and distant world, but the team was able to gather important information about its geology and atmosphere. The team returned to Earth with a wealth of new knowledge and data about the solar system. They shared their findings with other scientists, and soon, many more missions were planned to explore the depths of space.

**Pride is ego**

Alexander was proud of his royal heritage and believed that he was better than everyone else. He looked down on the commoners and thought they were beneath him. Alexander was out riding one day on horseback through the kingdom when he came across a poor farmer who was struggling to plow his field. The prince scoffed at the farmer and rode on without offering to help, as he continued on his journey, he came across a group of merchants who were stuck in the mud with their carts. Again, Alexander scoffed at them and rode on without offering any assistance.

As the day went on, Alexander became increasingly arrogant. He believed that he was above helping others and that they should be grateful for anything he designed to give them. But his pride was soon to be humbled, as he rode back to the palace that evening, he was ambushed by a group of bandits. They took him prisoner and demanded a ransom from the king for his safe return. The king, who loved his son dearly, paid the ransom, but Alexander was deeply humbled by his experience. He realized that his pride had blinded him to the needs of others and that he had been wrong to look down on them.

Alexander made it his mission from that time on to be a kind and compassionate ruler. He helped the poor, assisted the merchants, and made sure that everyone in the kingdom was taken care of. He learned that true strength comes from helping others and not from putting oneself above them. And in the end, he was loved by all.

**Fear**

Lucy had always been a brave and adventurous child, but as she grew older, she began to realize that there was one thing that she feared more than anything else in the world: the dark. As the sun set each evening, Lucy's heart would race with anxiety as the shadows began to creep into her room. She tried to tell herself that there was nothing to be afraid of, that it was just her imagination playing tricks on her, but the fear was always there, lurking just beneath the surface.

One night, as she lay in bed, unable to sleep because of her fear, Lucy decided that she couldn't take it anymore. She knew that she needed to face her fear head-on if she ever wanted to be free of it. So, with a deep breath, she got out of bed and walked to the door of her room. As she opened the door, the darkness seemed to swallow her whole. Her heart pounded in her chest as she took a step into the unknown. But as she walked further and further into the dark, she realized that there was nothing to be afraid of. The shadows were just shadows, and the things that she had imagined were hiding in the darkness were not real.

With a smile on her face, Lucy turned and walked back to her bed. As she lay down, she felt a sense of peace wash over her. From that day forward, she was no longer afraid of the dark. She knew that she could face anything, as long as she had the courage to do so.

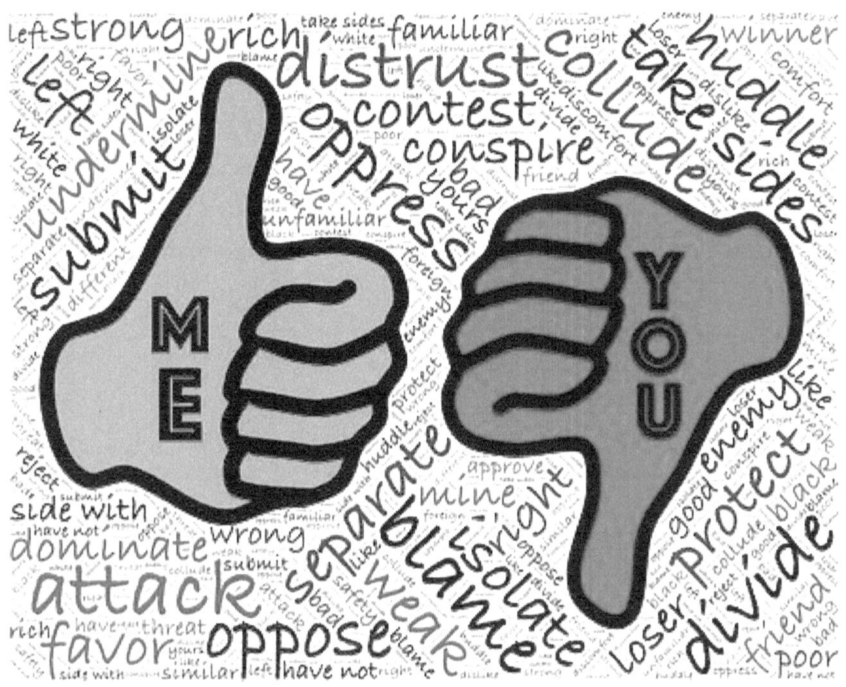


## Revenge of the Backstabbers

Jack worked hard to climb the ranks of his company, but he had a few colleagues who were not as supportive as he would have liked. These colleagues, known as "backstabbers," would often undermine Jack's efforts and take credit for his ideas.

Despite their constant sabotage, Jack continued to push forward and eventually landed a promotion to a high-level position within the company. His backstabbing colleagues were envious of his success and became even more determined to bring him down.

One day, they set a trap for Jack and convinced the company's top executives that he had stolen a valuable project from one of his colleagues. Jack was fired from his job and his reputation was ruined. Feeling betrayed and furious, Jack vowed to get revenge. He spent months gathering evidence and building a case against his former colleagues. He also worked hard to improve his skills and build a new network of contacts in the industry.

Finally, the day of reckoning arrived. Jack presented his evidence to the company's top executives and exposed his colleagues as the true thieves and backstabbers that they were. They were fired and their reputations were also ruined. Jack, meanwhile, landed a new job at a rival company with a higher salary and more prestige than his previous position. He had achieved his revenge and could finally put the past behind him and move forward with his career.

**Soul-Search**

Jenny had always been searching for true happiness, but never seemed to find it. She tried everything from material possessions to relationships, but nothing ever seemed to bring her the contentment she craved.

While out for a walk in the park, she came across an old wise man sitting on a bench. She sat down next to him and told him about her quest for true happiness. The wise man listened patiently and then told her, "True happiness cannot be found in things or people. It can only be found within yourself."

Jenny was skeptical but decided to give it a try. She began to focus on her inner self and started to practice mindfulness and meditation, making a conscious effort to be grateful for the things she had, rather than always wanting more.

Over time, Jenny began to notice a change in herself, as she felt more at peace and content with her life. She realized that true happiness was not something that could be found externally, but rather it was a state of being that she could cultivate within herself.

Jenny could now live a happy and fulfilling life being that she learned that true happiness is not something that can be bought or given, but something that is created from within. And she lived happily ever after.

**Honesty**

Mark had a reputation for being dishonest, always looking for ways to cheat and deceive others. He would lie to his friends and steal from the local merchants.

The town where he resided was struck by a terrible storm, and many of the houses were destroyed, including Mark's. The residents came together to help rebuild the homes, but Mark saw this as an opportunity to take advantage of their generosity. He told lies to receive more aid than he deserved, and even stole supplies from his neighbors.

As the town slowly regained its strength, the residents began to realize the extent of Mark's dishonesty. They no longer trusted him and he was shunned by the community. Feeling the weight of his actions, Mark finally realized the error of his ways, and he apologized to the residents and worked tirelessly to make amends for his past actions. He returned the stolen goods and helped rebuild the homes of those he had deceived.

Through his hard work and determination to be honest, Mark regained the trust and respect of his community. He became known for his integrity and was a valued member of the village.

Mark would later live his life with honesty and transparency and was an inspiration to all who knew him. He taught that honesty is the foundation of trust and that it is never too late to change for the better.

**Astrology**

Far off in a kingdom somewhere, there were twelve beautiful princesses, each born under a different zodiac sign.

The first princess, Aries, was fierce and independent. She was always the first to volunteer for adventures and was known for her courage and determination.

The second princess, Taurus, was strong-willed and practical. She loved to garden and was known for her green thumb.

The third princess, Gemini, was known for her intelligence and curiosity. She loved to read and was always eager to learn more about the world around her.

The fourth princess, Cancer, was kind and compassionate. She had a great love for animals and often rescued them from the forest.

The fifth princess, Leo, was proud and regal. She loved to dance and was known for her grace and poise.

The sixth princess, Virgo, was hardworking and organized. She loved to keep things tidy and was known for her attention to detail.

The seventh princess, Libra, was charming and diplomatic. She loved to make friends and was always able to settle disputes between her sisters.

The eighth princess, Scorpio, was mysterious and intense. She loved to study magic and was known for her powerful spells.

The ninth princess, Sagittarius, was optimistic and adventurous. She loved to travel and was always eager to explore new places.

The tenth princess, Capricorn, was ambitious and disciplined. She loved to set goals and was known for her determination to achieve them.

The eleventh princess, Aquarius, was unique and independent. She loved to invent and was known for her creative ideas.

The twelfth princess, Pisces, was sensitive and intuitive. She loved to paint and was known for her beautiful artwork.

One day, a terrible dragon threatened the kingdom, and the king called upon the twelve princesses to help defeat it. Each princess used her unique talents and strengths to help in the battle. Together, they were able to defeat the dragon and save the kingdom. From then on, the princesses were known as the "Zodiac Warriors" and their story was told for generations to come.

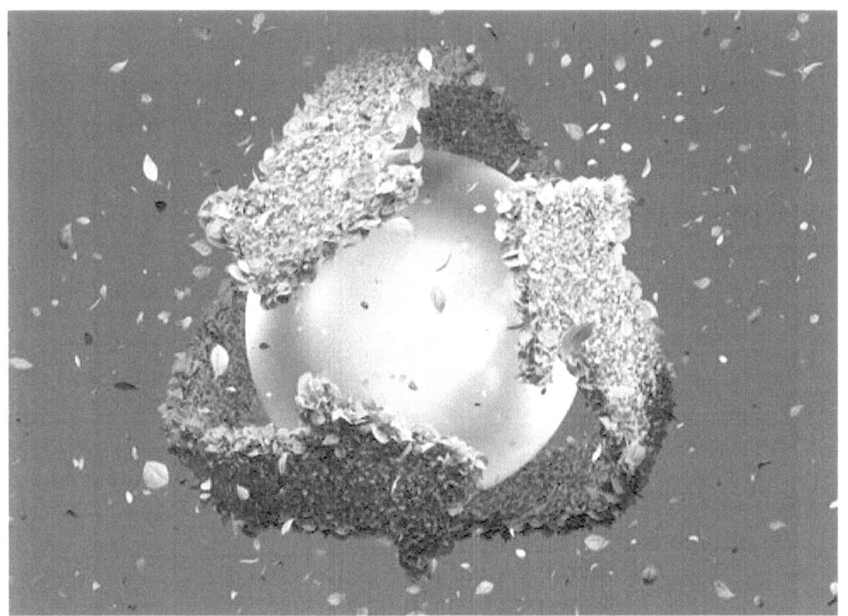

**Renewable**

There was a kingdom that relied heavily on fossil fuels for its energy needs. However, as time went by, the people of the kingdom started to realize the negative impact it was having on the environment. The air was polluted, the water was contaminated, and wildlife was suffering.

The king and his advisors were determined to find a solution to their energy problems. They brought in scientists and engineers from all over the world to help find clean energy sources that would be both sustainable and affordable for the kingdom.

After many months of research and development, the team of experts came up with a plan to harness the power of the sun, wind, and water to generate clean energy for the kingdom. The king was pleased with their work and immediately invested in the necessary infrastructure to implement the plan.

Solar panels were installed on rooftops and in fields, wind turbines were set up along the coast, and hydroelectric dams were built on the rivers. The kingdom was soon producing more energy than it could use and was even able to export excess energy to other countries.

The impact of this shift to clean energy was dramatic. The air became cleaner, the water became purer, and wildlife started to thrive once again. The people of the kingdom were proud of their leaders for making such a positive change and were grateful for the improved quality of life that came with it.

From that day on, the kingdom was known as a leader in clean energy and inspired other countries to follow in its footsteps. And so, the people of the kingdom lived happily ever after, with an abundant supply of clean, sustainable energy.

## Euphoria

Kate lived a monotonous life, always going through the motions and feeling unfulfilled. One day, she stumbled upon a magical potion that promised to bring her a feeling of euphoria like no other.

Curious, Kate drank the potion and was immediately transported to a world filled with pure bliss. Colors were brighter, music was sweeter, and laughter echoed through the air. She danced with joy, laughed with delight, and experienced happiness like she had never felt before.

However, as the effects of the potion began to wear off, Kate realized that this feeling of euphoria was not real. It was just a temporary escape from the mundane reality of her life. She knew that she could not rely on this potion forever and that she needed to find a way to bring joy and happiness into her everyday life.

So, Kate started to make small changes in her life. She began to appreciate the beauty in the simple things, like a sunset or a bird singing. She surrounded herself with positive people who uplifted and supported her. And most importantly, she learned to find joy within herself and to believe in her own worth and happiness.

With time, Kate found that the small changes she made had a big impact on her life. She was no longer dependent on the potion and found that she was able to experience feelings of euphoria on her own, just by living a fulfilling life filled with love, laughter, and positivity.

Kate went on to live a life filled with true happiness, grateful for the experience that taught her the true meaning of euphoria.

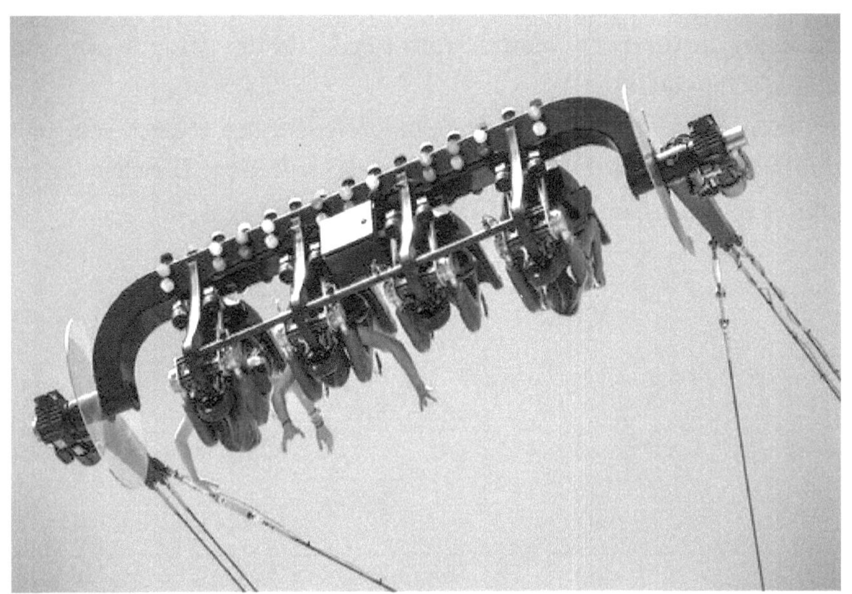

**Adrenaline**

There was a group of friends who loved adventure and thrills. They were known as adrenaline junkies and sought out any opportunity to get their heart racing.

One day, they decided to go skydiving for the first time. They were nervous but also incredibly excited. When they jumped out of the plane, they felt an instant rush of adrenaline as the wind whipped past their faces. It was the ultimate thrill, and they were hooked.

From that day on, they went on many more adventures, including bungee jumping, white water rafting, and even BASE jumping. They traveled all over the world, always searching for the next adrenaline rush.

But as they took more and more risks, they began to realize the importance of safety. They made sure to educate themselves and always use proper gear. They also started to appreciate the beauty and peace of the world around them, rather than just the thrills.

One day, they took a break from their adventures to go hiking in the mountains. As they climbed to the top and looked out at the breathtaking view, they realized that life is about balance. They could still enjoy the thrill of adventure, but also take the time to appreciate the simple things in life.

From then on, the adrenaline junkies continued to seek out new thrills, but also made time for relaxation and reflection. They lived their lives to the fullest and inspired others to do the same.

**Pet the Pets**

There was a girl named Ellen who loved animals. She had two pets, a dog named Max and a cat named Bella. Max was a playful golden retriever who loved to chase his tail and play fetch. Bella was a mischievous calico cat who loved to climb on things and play with string.

One day, Ellen learned about a local animal shelter that was in need of volunteers. She went to the shelter and started volunteering every weekend, playing with the dogs and cats and helping to clean their cages.

At the shelter, Ellen met a shy but sweet pup named Rusty. Rusty was a scruffy terrier mix who had been abandoned by his previous owner. Ellen fell in love with Rusty and convinced her parents to adopt him. Max and Bella were a little unsure about the new addition to their family, but after a few days of sniffing and playing, they became the best of friends.

Ellen and her pets spent their days exploring the park, playing in the backyard, and snuggling on the couch. Ellen loved her pets and was so grateful to have them in her life. She was happy to know that she had made a difference in Rusty's life and that he was no longer lonely.

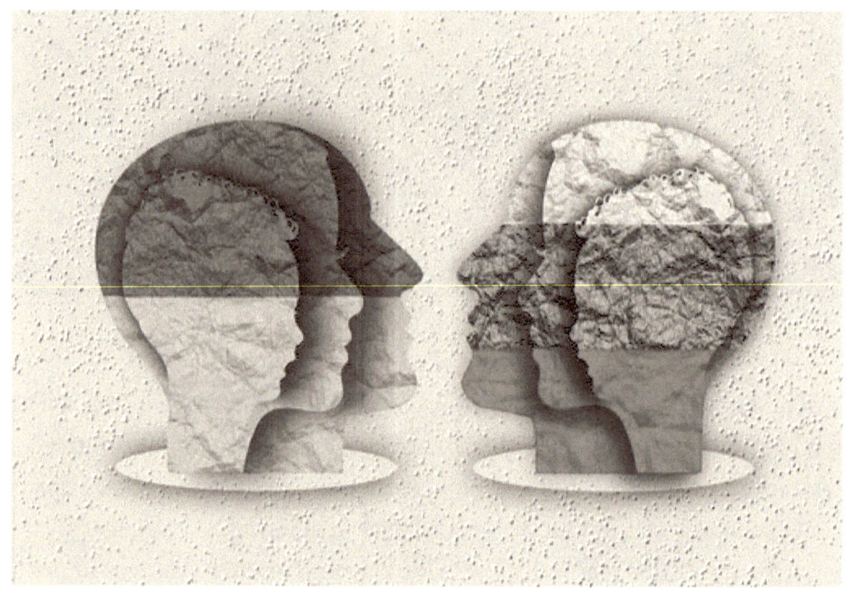

In 2014, tensions between Russia and Ukraine reached a boiling point when Russia annexed Crimea, a region of Ukraine that had significant cultural, historical, and strategic importance to Russia. The annexation was met with widespread international condemnation and led to the outbreak of a conflict in eastern Ukraine between Ukrainian government forces and pro-Russian separatists.

The root causes of the conflict can be traced back to the post-Soviet era, when Ukraine, like many other former Soviet republics, struggled to define its national identity and establish its place in the international community. In particular, Ukraine faced a choice between aligning itself with the West, which many Ukrainians saw as a path to greater prosperity and freedom, or with Russia, which they viewed as their historical and cultural homeland.

This struggle came to a head in 2014 when Ukraine's pro-Russian president was ousted by a popular uprising and replaced by a pro-Western government. Russia saw this as a threat to its strategic interests and an attempt by the West to encircle and weaken it. In response, Russia annexed Crimea, which had been part of Russia until 1954, and supported separatist forces in eastern Ukraine.

The conflict has since claimed the lives of thousands of people and caused a major humanitarian crisis in the region. Despite numerous ceasefires and peace agreements, the conflict remains unresolved, and the two sides are still far apart on key issues such as the status of the separatist regions and the future of Ukraine's relationship with Russia and the West.

The exact reasons for Russia's invasion of Ukraine in 2022 are not clear, but it is widely believed to be related to the political and territorial disputes between the two countries. Some believe that Russia sought to regain control over Crimea and other parts of Ukraine, while others suggest that the invasion was a power grab aimed at asserting Russian dominance in the region.

In conclusion, the conflict between Russia and Ukraine was caused by a complex mixture of historical, cultural, strategic, and geopolitical factors, and its resolution will require a delicate balance of interests and compromises.

**Seeing the best**

Maria lived in a small village and, despite the many flaws and faults of the villagers, Maria always saw the best in them ignoring their shortcomings.

The village would come in peril as a fierce dragon threatened to destroy everything. Everyone was frightened and didn't know what to do, but Maria stepped forward and offered to go and talk to the dragon.

The villagers were skeptical, but Maria was undeterred. She approached the dragon and instead of fighting, she began to talk to it. To everyone's surprise, the dragon wasn't evil after all but was simply misunderstood.

With her kind words and understanding, Maria was able to convince the dragon to leave the village in peace. The dragon became a friend to the village and protected it from any harm.

The villagers were grateful to Maria for her bravery and for seeing the best in the dragon, even when no one else could. They learned to do the same, to see the best in each other, and to overlook their flaws.

From that day on, the village was a happy place where everyone lived in harmony, all thanks to Maria's unwavering belief in the goodness of others.

**School**

Kelly felt the pressure of school every day. She had high expectations from her parents, who wanted her to get straight A's and be at the top of her class. Sarah also felt the pressure of fitting in with her peers and the constant comparison on social media.

She struggled to balance her homework, extracurricular activities, and personal life. Kelly often found herself staying up late to finish assignments and sacrificing time with her family and friends. The pressure to succeed weighed heavy on her shoulders, causing her to feel overwhelmed and stressed.

One day, Kelly met with her teacher who noticed her struggling and asked her how she was doing. Kelly opened up about the pressure she was feeling and her teacher listened and offered support. The teacher encouraged Sarah to prioritize self-care and focus on her mental health, explaining that academic success is not everything.

Kelly took the advice to heart and started to set realistic goals for herself. She learned to say no to activities that didn't bring her joy and prioritized spending time with her loved ones. She also found healthy coping mechanisms to manage her stress, such as journaling and practicing mindfulness.

As a result, Kelly's grades improved and she felt more confident and content. She realized that the pressure to succeed is a common experience for many students, but it's important to remember to take care of oneself and find a healthy balance.

**At The End Of The Tunnel**

There were a group of individuals who felt lost and hopeless, wandering through a dark endless tunnel with no idea where they were headed. The journey was long and tiring, but they trudged on, searching for a glimmer of hope.

One day, they spotted a faint light in the distance. The light seemed small and far away, but it was enough to give the person a spark of inspiration. They picked up their pace and began to run toward the light.

As they got closer, the light grew brighter and brighter. The group felt a sense of comfort and hope as they ran toward it. Finally, they reached the end of the tunnel and emerged into a bright, beautiful world. The sun was shining and the sky was a brilliant blue.

The group stood there in awe, taking in the beauty around them. They finally realized that the light they had seen was the light of hope. The light that had guided them out of the dark and into the beauty of the world. They knew that they would never be lost again, as long as they held on to that light.

The group lived a happy and fulfilling life, always remembering the light that had led them out of the tunnel, and whenever they faced a difficult situation, they would think back to that day and remember the light that had given them hope. They knew that as long as they had hope, they could find their way through even the darkest of tunnels.

**Cooking is like science in many ways:**

1. Both involve experimenting and testing.
2. Both rely on precise measurements and accuracy.
3. Both use principles of chemistry and physics (e.g. heat transfer, acid-base reactions).
4. Both strive to understand and replicate outcomes through repeatable processes.
5. Both can lead to new discoveries and innovations.

Cooking and science both involve experimentation and a systematic approach to achieving a desired result. In cooking, the cook adjusts ingredients and cooking methods to create a tasty dish, while in science, a researcher manipulates variables to test a hypothesis and arrive at a conclusion. Both also require attention to detail, precise measurements, and a willingness to iterate and make improvements based on the results.

**Self-Improvement**

David felt unfulfilled in life, didn't know what his purpose was, and often felt lost and sad. David came across a book about self-improvement and decided to give it a try. He learned about setting goals, exercising regularly, eating well, and surrounding himself with positive people.

At first, it was challenging for David to stick to these new habits, but he was determined to make a change in his life. He started by setting small, achievable goals, like waking up earlier and taking a walk each morning.

As he accomplished these goals, David felt more confident and energized. He then set larger goals, such as learning a new skill or traveling to a new place. With hard work and dedication, David achieved each of these goals, one by one.

Along the way, David also made new friends who supported and encouraged him. He felt a new sense of purpose and happiness.

In the end, David realized that self-improvement was a never-ending journey. He was always striving to become a better version of himself and was grateful for the changes he had made in his life.

David was now able to live a life filled with joy, purpose, and fulfillment.

### Relations and Compromise

A couple named Fran and Teddy. They had been together for a few years and things were going well. However, they had begun to experience some difficulties in their relationship.

Teddy loved to go out and party, while Fran preferred to stay at home and relax. This led to many arguments and disagreements between them. They both wanted to be happy, but their interests and lifestyles were completely different.

One day, they decided to sit down and talk about their differences. They both agreed that relationships were about compromise and that they needed to find a way to make things work between them.

They came up with a plan. Teddy would go out and party once a week, while Fran would accompany him for one night a month. This way, they could both enjoy their interests and spend quality time together.

With this new agreement, they both felt happier and more satisfied with their relationship. They learned that by compromising and finding a middle ground, they could maintain their individual interests while also making each other happy.

Going forward, they lived a life filled with love, laughter, and happiness. They had finally discovered the true meaning of compromise in relationships and they never looked back.

**Risk**

Max in living a comfortable life but felt unfulfilled. He longed for excitement and adventure but was too afraid of taking risks.

One day, he met an old man who told him a story about a treasure hidden in a distant land, beyond a treacherous mountain range. The old man said that many had tried to find the treasure, but only a few who were brave enough to take risks had succeeded.

Max was inspired by the story and decided to set out on an adventure to find the treasure. He knew that it wouldn't be easy, but the reward would be worth it.

He encountered many obstacles along the way, including dangerous animals, harsh weather, and treacherous terrain. But, with determination and a willingness to take risks, Max persevered.

Finally, after months of traveling, he reached the entrance to the hidden cave where the treasure was said to be kept. He took a deep breath and stepped inside, facing his biggest fear head-on.

And there it was, the treasure that he had sought for so long. It was more magnificent than he had ever imagined, filled with gold, jewels, and rare artifacts.

Max realized that the greatest reward of taking risks was not the treasure itself, but the personal growth and confidence he had gained along the way. He had learned that life was meant to be lived to the fullest and that taking risks was the only way to truly experience all it had to offer.

Max lived a life full of adventures and excitement, never again afraid to take risks. And he knew that the greatest reward of all was the journey, not the destination.

**If they don't, believe in YOU**

Lily had a big dream of becoming a famous singer and had a beautiful voice, with a passion for music, but every time she performed in front of others, she was met with criticism and negativity.

Her classmates would laugh and make fun of her, saying she was tone-deaf and had no future in music. Her parents and siblings also discouraged her, saying it was a waste of time and that she should focus on more practical pursuits.

Despite all of this negativity, Lily refused to give up on her dream. She knew deep down that she had a gift and was determined to make it a reality.

She started practicing in secret, spending hours each day perfecting her skills. Slowly but surely, her confidence grew and her voice became stronger.

One day, Lily entered a local singing competition. The judges were amazed by her talent and declared her the winner. The audience was in awe of her performance, and she received a standing ovation.

After that night, Lily became a local celebrity, and her name was soon known throughout the country. People who once laughed at her now sought her out for autographs and performances.

Lily never forgot the people who had put her down, but she never let their negativity get to her. Instead, she remained focused on her goal and let her talents and hard work speak for themselves.

In the end, Lily's persistence paid off. She went on to become a famous singer, traveling the world and performing for sold-out crowds. She never forgot the importance of believing in herself, and she inspired countless others to do the same.

**Driver**

Takahiro loved to drive, as he believed that driving reflected his personality and that he could tell a lot about a person by the way they drove.

Takahiro was a confident and bold driver who would speed down the roads and take sharp turns, always pushing his limits, always in control, and never afraid of taking risks.

On the other hand, Takahiro's best friend, Akane, was a much more cautious driver. She always followed the rules of the road and made sure to leave plenty of space between her and other cars. She was patient and calmed behind the wheel, and never let her emotions get the best of her.

One day, Takahiro and Akane went on a road trip together. Takahiro wanted to show off his driving skills and impress Akane, but she was more interested in enjoying the scenery and getting to their destination safely.

As they drove, Takahiro realized that Akane's driving style reflected her personality just as much as he did. She was a thoughtful and considerate person who always put others first, and her driving reflected that.

Takahiro also realized that everyone has different driving styles, just as everyone has different personalities. Some people are confident and bold, while others are more cautious and reserved. But no matter what, each person's driving style is a reflection of who they are and what they value.

Takahiro appreciated the diversity of driving styles and understood that they are all valid, just like the diverse personalities that make up the world.

**Fashionista**

Janet loved fashion, spending hours every day getting dressed in the latest trends and admiring herself in the mirror. She was the most fashionable person in the neighborhood, and everyone admired her for her unique sense of style. One day, while she was out shopping for new clothes, she met an old wise man. The old man asked her why she was so obsessed with fashion, and Janet replied that she wanted to look good and feel confident. The old man smiled and said, "Fashion is important, but it's not everything. It's just a small part of who you are, and it shouldn't define you."

Janet was taken aback by the old man's words, and she realized that she had been focusing too much on her appearance and not enough on who she was as a person. She decided to spend more time doing things that made her happy, like reading, writing, and playing music. She also started helping others, volunteering at the local shelter spending time with her friends and family. As she started to focus more on what was truly important, Janet began to glow from the inside out. She no longer felt the need to dress up every day to feel good about herself, and she started to appreciate the simple things in life. People started to notice the change in her and admired her for her kindness and compassion, not just for her fashion sense.

Janet learned that fashion is important, but it's not everything. What truly matters is who you are as a person, and what you do with your life. She lived happily ever after, spreading joy and happiness wherever she went. The story shows that while fashion is important and can make us feel good, it's not everything. It's important to focus on what truly matters, and to be kind, compassionate, and to live a life filled with joy and happiness.

**Never just a book by its cover**

There was an old and worn-out book that no one wanted to read. The cover was torn and faded, and the pages were yellow with age. The library patrons often passed by the book and would say, "Who would want to read such an old and ugly book?"

One day, a curious young boy named Kevin decided to take a look at the book. He was tired of hearing the villagers judge the book by its cover, and wanted to see for himself what was inside.

Kevin was surprised to find that the book was filled with exciting adventures and beautiful illustrations. The words were written in a language that was new to him, but he was determined to understand it. He spent hours reading the book, lost in its world of magic and wonder.

The employees of the library were shocked to see Kevin so engrossed in the book. They had never seen him so happy and eager to learn. They came to the realization that they had been judging the book by its cover and that there was much more to it than they had thought.

The book would be discovered to be an artifact from a King that had once ruled and with news of Kevin reading the book based on a news broadcast, people would seek out Kevin to ask him about the book and what he had learned from it. They were amazed by all the knowledge and wisdom he had gained from reading it.

Kevin taught them that it's never a good idea to judge a book by its cover and that there's always more to something than meets the eye. He showed them that the real value of a book is in the knowledge and inspiration that can be gained from its pages.

The book became a treasured item in the library, and generations of children learned excerpts from it, just as Kevin had. And so, the lesson of not judging a book by its cover was passed down from generation to generation.

www.ingramcontent.com/pod-product-compliance
Lightning Source LLC
LaVergne TN
LVHW090125160826
845673LV00015B/1025
*9789356468900*